# The Mommy Book

Published by Silver Press,
A Division of Simon & Schuster
299 Jefferson Road, Parsippany, New Jersey 07054

Designed by Studio Goodwin Sturges

Manufactured in the United States of America
10 9 8 7 6 5 4 3 2 1

Library of Congress Cataloging-in-Publication Data
Morris, Ann, 1930-
The mommy book/by Ann Morris: photographs by Ken Heyman.
p. cm.—(The World's Family series)
Summary:  Photographs of mothers around the world depict a
positive look at the relationship between mothers and children.
1. Mothers—Juvenile literature.  2. Mothers and children
—Juvenile literature.  [1. Mother and child.]  I. Heyman, Ken, ill.
II. Title.  III. Series.
HQ759.M865  1996
306.874'3—dc20   95-12237   CIP   AC
ISBN 0-382-24692-6 (JHC)    ISBN 0-382-24693-4 (LSB)
ISBN 0-382-24694-2 (PBK)

# The Mommy Book

By Ann Morris
Photographs by Ken Heyman

Silver Press
Parsippany, New Jersey

Mommies take good care of you

before you were born
and when you were a tiny baby.

# They wash you

and feed you

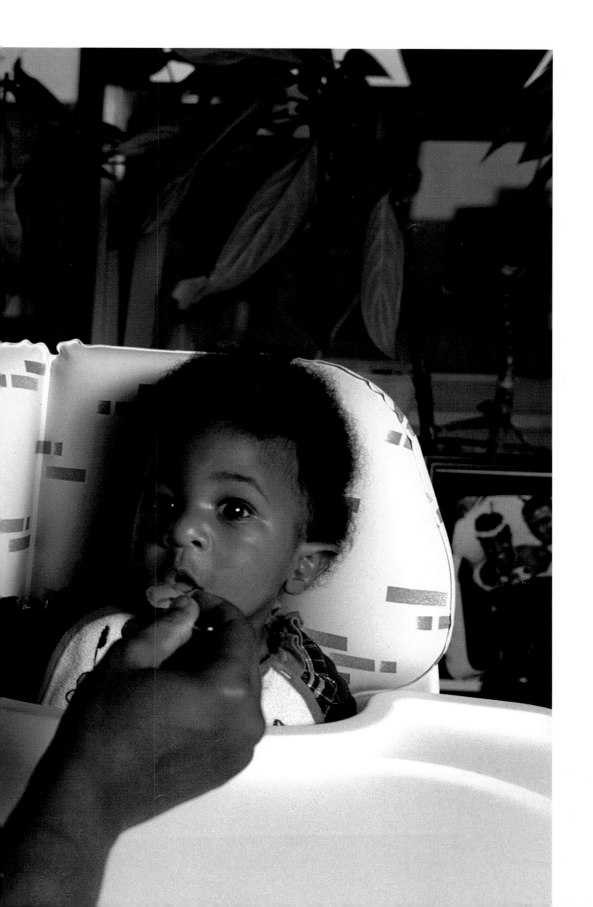

and teach you to cook, too.

They read you stories.

# They help you write letters.

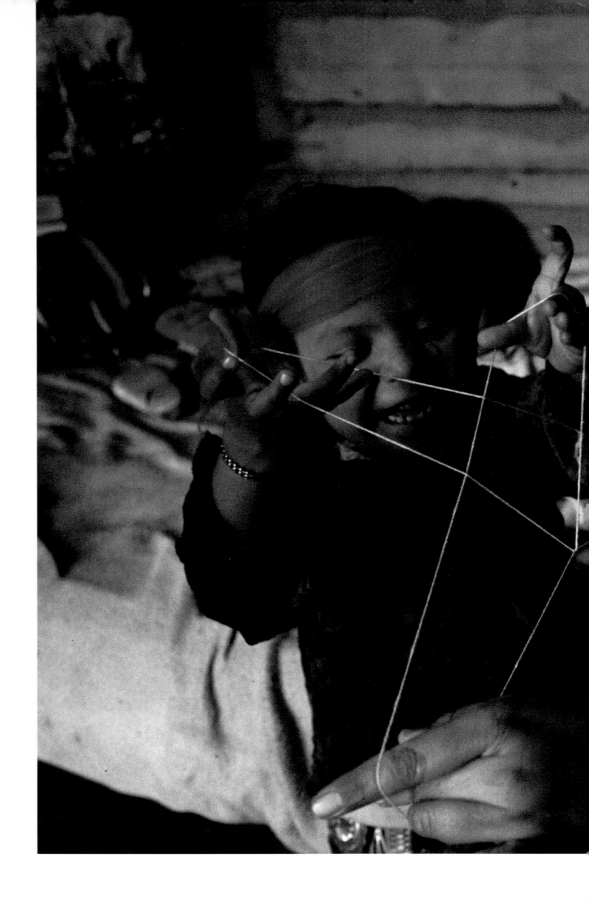

Mommies are fun to play with

everywhere . . .

in the park . . .

and stringing popcorn by the fire.

# Mommies are sometimes called "Mom."

Moms and mommies are
an important part of a family.

Grandmas are an
important part of a family too.

Some grandmas are called "Granny" or "Nana." What do you call yours?

Some mommies go to an office to work.

Or sell things in a market.

But wherever you live,

mommies help you
when you're feeling bad or scared.

Mommies are there for you
when you need them

with loving talk, hugs,
and a big smile.

# Index to Mommies

**Page 18:** This mom shows her family how to string popcorn and cranberries to hang on the tree.

**Page 20:** On a sleepy Sunday morning, a mom and her family enjoy a book together before they go off to see Grandma.

**Page 21:** On market day in Guatemala, these children stay with their mother. She sells rugs to make a living.

**Page 22:** Grandmothers enjoy special time with their grandchildren. Grandmothers have an important place in every family.

**Page 24:** Sometimes this little girl misses her mom when her mom is at work.

**Page 25:** In a Moroccan market, it is late in the day when this mom is selling the last of her lemons.

**Page 26:** In Italy, Grandma spins the wool into thread while the little boy's mother comforts him after he has fallen down.

**Page 28:** This boy from Wisconsin gets a special hug from his mom.

**Page 29:** This mom and her son play in Central Park in New York City. The boy's hair is short because of his religion.

# Ann Morris

Ann Morris's many books for children include **Bread Bread Bread, Hats Hats Hats, How Teddy Bears Are Made** and **Dancing to America**. She has been a teacher in public and private schools and has taught courses in language arts, children's literature, and writing for children at Bank Street College, Teachers College, Queens College of the City University of New York, and at The New School in New York City.

# Ken Heyman

Ken Heyman's photographic career has taken him into the heart of many indigenous cultures. His photographs have appeared in publications such as **Life, Look,** and **The New York Times**, and his work has been exhibited on three continents. His photographs illustrate numerous children's books, and he is the co-author of **Family** with Margaret Mead. He lives in New York City.